KUMAK'S HOUSE

A Tale of the Far North

Michael Bania

Alaska Northwest Books™

At the edge of a great frozen river,
Kumak and his family lived in their house by the willows.

2

Though their house was warm and cozy,
Kumak was not happy.

His wife
was not happy.

His wife's mother
was not happy.

His sons and daughters
were not happy.

"Too small, this house," said Kumak.

"I will go see Aana Lulu. She will know what to do."

Aana Lulu was the oldest and wisest elder in the village. Kumak had great respect for her. She had once made a wart on Kumak's hand shrivel and die.

At her house Kumak asked, "Aana Lulu, what can I do? My house is too small. My wife is unhappy. My wife's mother is unhappy. My sons and daughters are unhappy."

"Ahhh, Kumak," said Aana Lulu, sewing fine stitches around the top of a sealskin mukluk. "Unhappy is the mukluk on too big a foot. Go to the trees and find Rabbit. Invite Rabbit to live with you."

And Kumak did.

He hitched up his dog team
and mushed over the icy tundra to the trees.
He brought Rabbit and her family
back to share his house.

7

"Just right," said Rabbit.

"Still too small, this house," sighed Kumak.

"I will go see Aana Lulu again."

"Aana," begged Kumak. "Nothing has changed. My wife is unhappy. My wife's mother is unhappy. My sons and daughters are unhappy. On the other hand, Rabbit is perfectly happy."

"Ahhh, Kumak," said Aana Lulu, scraping a muskrat skin for the sleeve of a parka. "Unhappy is the parka on too big a body. Go to the lake and find Fox in the willows. Invite Fox to live with you."

And Kumak did.

"Just right," said Fox.

"This house," grumbled Kumak, "still too small."
"I will go see Aana Lulu at the first light of day."

"Aana Lulu," begged Kumak. "My house is getting smaller. My wife is unhappy. My wife's mother is unhappy. My sons and daughters are unhappy. On the other hand, Rabbit and Fox are perfectly happy."

"Ahhh, Kumak," said Aana Lulu, kneading enough dough for one hundred doughnuts. "Unhappy is the bowl with too much dough. Go to the mountains and find Caribou. Invite Caribou to live with you."

And Kumak did.

"Just right," said Caribou.

"This house is getting smaller instead of bigger," groaned Kumak.

"I will go to Aana Lulu's one more time."

"Aana Lulu," begged Kumak. "My house is smaller still. My wife is unhappy. My wife's mother is unhappy. My sons and daughters are unhappy. On the other hand, Rabbit, Fox, and Caribou are perfectly happy."

"Ahhh, Kumak," said Aana Lulu, picking leaves and twigs from a pail of frozen salmonberries. "Unhappy is the bush with too many berries. Go past Fish River and find Porcupine. Invite Porcupine to live with you."

And Kumak did.

Porcupine was so pleased that
he invited his friend Otter and Otter's family
to live at Kumak's house too.

"Just right," they said.

"Still too small," Kumak said
to himself. "I will go
back to Aana Lulu's
tomorrow."

"Aana Lulu," begged Kumak the next day. "What is happening to my house? My wife is unhappy. My wife's mother is unhappy. My sons and daughters are unhappy. On the other hand, Rabbit, Fox, Caribou, Porcupine, and Otter are perfectly happy."

"Ahhh, Kumak," said Aana Lulu, slicing blubber into small chunks for boiling. "Unhappy is the pot with too much soup. Go to the fork in the river and find Bear sleeping in her winter den. Invite Bear to live with you."

And Kumak did.

"Just right," said Bear.

Kumak's eyes bulged out of his head.

"This house is so small, there is barely room for us!" he roared.

He grabbed his beaver hat and ran like the West Wind to Aana Lulu's house.

"Aana! Please do something," begged Kumak. "Instead of getting bigger, my house keeps getting smaller! My wife is unhappy. My wife's mother is unhappy. My sons and daughters are unhappy. On the other hand, Rabbit, Fox, Caribou, Porcupine, Otter, and Bear are perfectly happy."

"Ahhh, Kumak," said Aana Lulu, carefully cutting the last piece for a beaver hat. "Unhappy is the hat on too big a head. Go to the mouth of the river and look for Whale in the open water. Invite Whale to live with you."

And Kumak did.

"Just right," said Whale.

"TOO SMALL, THIS HOUSE!" bellowed Kumak all the way to Aana Lulu's house.

"Aana, help! My wife is very unhappy. My wife's mother is very unhappy. My sons and daughters are very unhappy. On the other hand, Rabbit, Fox, Caribou, Porcupine, Otter, Bear, and Whale are perfectly happy!"

"Ahhh, Kumak," said Aana Lulu, weaving grasses into a splendid basket. "Your guests have stayed too long. Send them away this very night!"

And Kumak did!

Kumak's wife was happy. His wife's mother was happy.
His sons and daughters were happy. And Kumak was happy too.

"Just right, this house," he said.

Author's Note about the Story

If you want to know where Kumak and his family live, put your finger on the left side of a map of Alaska starting with the long "tusk" of the Aleutian Islands. Go north, up along the coast until you get to the Arctic Circle. Follow the Arctic Circle inland to the right just a little, and below that is the village of Buckland on the Buckland River. Buckland is one of 11 villages that make up the Northwest Arctic.

I lived in the Arctic for 17 years, and Buckland was my home for 9 of those years. My husband, our son, and I lived in this Eskimo village of about 450 people. I was "Teacher Michael" for 5 years.

Eskimos have a long tradition of storytelling. My kindergarten and prekindergarten students loved to hear the stories their elders told. At school they especially enjoyed traditional folktales similar to *Kumak's House*. I thought it would be fun for the children to read a book with a familiar story that took place in their own village. So I created *Kumak's House*.

Life in Buckland centers around the river. During the short summer, the children play and swim in the river. But for eight months of the year, the river is frozen hard and the ice is so thick that you can easily walk across it to find the best hills for sliding. The winter months are cold and dark. Luckily for Kumak, this story takes place in spring when the days are getting longer but the snow and ice still have two more months before melting. This is the best time for racing dog teams, riding snowmobiles, and traveling across the tundra and frozen rivers.

When Aana (pronounced AH-na) Lulu sends Kumak (KOO-muk) to get an animal to invite home, he has to hitch up his dogs and sled and pull on his warmest mukluks and parka lined with fur. He then travels 15 or 20 miles over the snow and ice and back again.

If you were to visit a house like Kumak's, it would be full of people. Friends and relatives are always stopping by to visit and drink coffee. Lots of children run in and out. It is not uncommon in an Eskimo village for the grandparents to live with their children and grandchildren. The *aanas* and *taatas* (the grandmothers and grandfathers) are the village elders who pass down their knowledge of the old ways to the next generations. One of the most important values in the Northwest Arctic region is "Respect For Elders," and that is why Kumak always listens to Aana Lulu's wise suggestions.

Each time Kumak visits Aana Lulu, she is busy with one of many traditional activities that are practiced by women in the village today. These include skin-sewing; gathering, storing, and preparing traditional foods; basket-making and other subsistence activities.

When Kumak first goes to visit Aana Lulu on page 6, she is sewing mukluks, which are pull-on footwear usually made of caribou skin or sealskin. The fur can be on the inside or the outside. Mukluks are often decorated at the top with fur or small pieces of skin sewn with intricate patterns. When you need extra warmth, you can put a pair of caribou socks inside them. They are very warm, much better than snow boots.

On page 10, Aana Lulu is preparing muskrat skins with a homemade tool called an *itchuun*, which is used to scrape the skins soft. She will need over 100 small skins to make a man's parka. She will sew the skins together to fit the pattern. It takes a lot of practice to sew skins and not pull the hairs through to the wrong side. Girls in the village start learning skin-sewing skills when they are young.

On page 14, Aana Lulu is getting ready to make Eskimo doughnuts by shaping the yeast dough by hand into doughnut shapes. Eskimo doughnuts are similar to Indian fry bread and they are delicious. They are usually made for special occasions such as feasts, potlucks, birthdays, holidays, and funerals.

Berry-picking is a favorite fall season activity for women and children. On page 18, Aana Lulu is picking through a bucket of berries that were frozen for winter storage. If berries are picked on a windy day, they can be slowly poured from one container to another and the wind will blow away the stems and leaves, saving Aana Lulu extra work later in the winter. Blueberries, arctic blackberries, salmonberries, and cranberries will be eaten separately or mixed together.

On page 22, Kumak is looking through the steam from a pot of boiling whale blubber or muktuk that Aana Lulu is slicing. She is using an *ulu* or a woman's knife. Beluga whales are occasionally harvested at the mouth of the river and each family in the village receives an equal share of the catch. Chunks of muktuk from bowhead whales are sometimes received from relatives who live in coastal villages. The blubber is boiled to soften it, then small pieces are dipped in seal oil and eaten. A little goes a long way, as it is high in fat and vitamin A, and tastes very rich.

The Arctic has a few atmospheric phenomena that most children in the Lower 48 states will rarely see. A "sundog," like the one seen on pages 2 and 23, is a spectacular bright halo around the sun. Sundogs are formed as sunlight is refracted by ice crystals. The northern lights seen on pages 28 and 29 are frequently viewed in the Arctic when the nights are very cold and clear. Northern lights, or the *aurora borealis*, are usually white but can be green, red, and violet. Eskimo children pretend that they can call the northern lights by whistling.

When it is cold, you need to wear the right clothes in the Arctic. Beaver hats are the most common hat for very cold weather. In school, older children are taught how to make these hats using rabbit or fox fur, although beaver skins are the warmest. Many aanas sew beaver hats and mukluks before the holidays. It is a lucky boy or girl who receives such a gift at the village Christmas program.

Buckland is one of the few places in the Arctic where grass baskets are made. The special grasses grow near the mouth of the river and must be picked at just the right time and kept frozen in bundles. Making baskets requires patience and a sure hand to keep the stitches tight and even. While weaving baskets, the grasses must be kept constantly wet with water to keep them from becoming brittle. Only a few women in the village make these traditional baskets and they are beautiful.

At the end of the story, Kumak's family celebrates with their favorite foods: caribou or moose soup, Eskimo doughnuts, muktuk, seal oil, and berries. Life is *"just right"* in the Arctic.

Dedicated to the aanas of the Arctic whom I have known in Buckland, Shungnak, and Noatak. Taikuu!

A special thanks to my husband, John, who believes the Arctic to be the most beautiful place on earth and wanted all the details to be accurate. Also to my son, Buck, who was born above the Arctic Circle and whose excellent comments and suggestions were always appreciated. Thank you!

Text and illustrations © 2002 by Michael Bania
Published by Alaska Northwest Books™
An imprint of Graphic Arts Center Publishing Co.
P.O. Box 10306, Portland, Oregon 97296-0306
503/226-2402; www.gacpc.com

Library of Congress Cataloging-in-Publication Data

Available upon request.

Hardbound ISBN 0-88240-540-3
Softbound ISBN 0-88240-541-1

President/Publisher: Charles M. Hopkins
Associate Publisher: Douglas A. Pfeiffer
Editorial Staff: Timothy W. Frew,
   Ellen Harkins Wheat, Tricia Brown,
   Jean Andrews, Kathy Matthews,
   Jean Bond-Slaughter
Production Staff: Richard L. Owsiany,
   Susan Dupere
Design: Constance Bollen, CB Graphics

Printed on acid- and chlorine-free paper
in Singapore